Better Homes and Gardens®

A Tree Full Of Friends

First Edition. First Printing
ISBN: 0-696-01910-8

Marci watched the moving van pull away from her new house. "I wish we hadn't moved," she said to her brother, Max. "I miss my friends."

"I know, but you'll make new friends here," Max said. "I saw lots of kids when we drove in."

"I don't want to make new friends," Marci said. "And I don't like this place."

"You will after you get to know some people," Max said. "I'm going to go look for some kids."

BOOKS
MARCI'S
ROOM

Marci watched Max disappear around the corner. Then, she went up to her new room. It was smaller than her old room, and she didn't like the wallpaper. When she looked out the window all she could see were leaves. There was a huge willow tree in her backyard.

"There's no place to play," Marci said. "That big old tree takes up too much room." Suddenly she heard a giggle. "The tree just laughed! It must be alive."

"Of course I'm alive," a voice said. "Dead trees don't talk."

Marci ran outside and looked down the street. Max was nowhere in sight.

Marci crept around the house and stared at the tree. Then, standing as tall as she could, she said, "Don't you scare me, tree. Or I'll have my brother cut you down."

"Wait! You can't cut down the tree!" There was a loud crack, and someone came crashing through the branches to land at Marci's feet.

"Who are you?" Marci asked.

The girl brushed leaves from her hair. "Hi! I'm Sara Jo. This is my favorite climbing tree."

"I'm Marci, and I don't *like* to climb trees."

All of a sudden two kids tumbled out from under the branches. Marci jumped out of the way.

"That's Gus and Arnie," Sara Jo said. "They're twins."

"Do you really want to cut down our tree?" asked Gus.

"Yes. It fills up my whole yard. There's no place to play."

"This tree is a great place to play," said Arnie. "It's our clubhouse. We're the Willow Tree Pals."

"But, I like to play pretend," Marci said.

"We do, too," Gus said. "Come inside and see."

Marci followed the others as Gus held aside some low-hanging branches to make a door. Marci stepped through the opening and looked around.

Arnie scrambled up the tree trunk and hung upside down from a branch. "You're in a circus tent. Can you see it?"

Marci closed her eyes. When she opened them, she saw a striped tent. "Yes, I do!"

"Arnie and I are famous trapeze artists," Gus shouted. He swung through the air and caught another branch with his hands. "Come on up," he yelled.

"I can't," Marci cried. "That's too *high*."

Just then someone swept aside the branches and came under the tree. "Who's this?" she asked, looking at Marci. "She's not a member of our club."

"It's OK, Vera," Sara Jo said. "Marci just moved here, and our clubhouse is in her yard."

Vera flipped her long, fuzzy ears over her shoulders.

"I'm an actress. I just love to put on plays. This tree makes a perfect theater." She turned to Marci. "Can you act?"

"I . . . I don't think so," Marci said. "I've never tried."

"You don't have to play the lead," Vera said. "After all, I'm the star."

"I don't think I could be in a play at all," Marci said. "I'd be too scared."

POPCORN
¢5

Vera stuck her nose in the air. "Then I guess you can't be in our club. We'll move our clubhouse to somebody else's yard."

"But Vera," Sara Jo said, "Elliot and Bruno don't act in your plays. They make all the snacks to sell at intermission. Maybe Marci could help them."

"We don't need any more help," Bruno grumbled.

"That's right," Elliot agreed. "Anyway, Bruno eats the snacks as fast as we make them."

Marci tried to hold back her tears. "I knew I'd never be able to make new friends here."

Sara Jo took Marci aside. "You said you liked to play pretend, didn't you?"

Marci nodded.

"Well, being in a play is the same thing. Try to think of something we could all pretend together."

At first, Marci couldn't think of anything. Then, as she looked harder at the tree, she began to see . . . .

"A castle!" Marci shouted. "The tree is a beautiful castle, and we're in the ballroom. Can you see it?"

"I can," said Elliot, admiring the bright banners along the ballroom walls.

"Me, too," said Sara Jo.

Vera frowned. "I don't see a castle at all."

"Me neither," snorted Bruno.

"But Vera," said Marci. "You're wearing a beautiful dress, and you have a diamond crown on your head. You must be the queen."

"Hmm . . . ," Vera said. She adjusted the crown between her long, fuzzy ears. "It *is* beginning to look like a castle."

"Not to me," grunted Bruno.

"We need you outside the castle to protect it, Bruno," said Marci.

Bruno looked puzzled. "Me?"

"Yes. You're the big, strong castle guard."

Bruno stuck out his chest, picked up his shield, and marched outside to guard the castle.

"Who are we?" Gus asked.

"The court jesters," said Marci. "You make everybody laugh."

"Can we have bells on our toes?" squeaked Arnie, cartwheeling by Gus.

"Sure," said Marci.

Vera glanced around the castle. "We need a king."

"Not me," Elliot said. "I'm a knight."
"Me, too," said Sara Jo.
Suddenly there was a shout from outside the castle. "Halt! Who goes there?" asked Bruno.
Sara Jo pulled out her sword. "Bruno's trying to scare somebody off. Let's help."
Marci peeked out of the castle. "It's my brother with some more kids. I'm in here, Max! We're playing castle."
"That sounds like fun," Max said. "Can we play?"
"Of course," Vera said. "You're so tall, Max. You can be the king."
Max blushed as a golden crown appeared on his head.

Max and Marci and their new friends had a wonderful time playing under the willow tree.

"Now do you like it better here, Marci?" Max asked.

Marci smiled. "Well, I still miss my old friends, but I like my new friends, too. But you know what I like best of all?"

"What?" asked Max.

"We have a friendship tree right here in our own backyard!"

Picture Frame House

Put your picture on a folded paper frame and give it to a friend.

What you'll need...

- One 8x8-inch piece of construction paper or other medium-weight paper
- Buttons
- 1 small paper doily
- House Trims (see page 32)
- 1 photograph

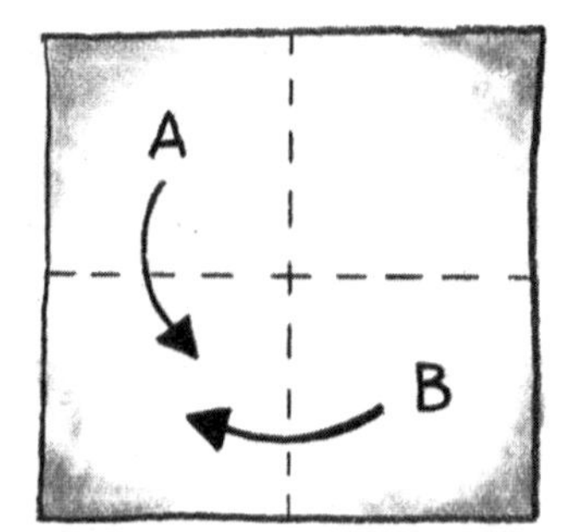

1 Fold the paper in half (A), then unfold. Fold the paper in half the other way (B), then unfold.

2 Fold the top edge just to the center crease. Turn the paper over.

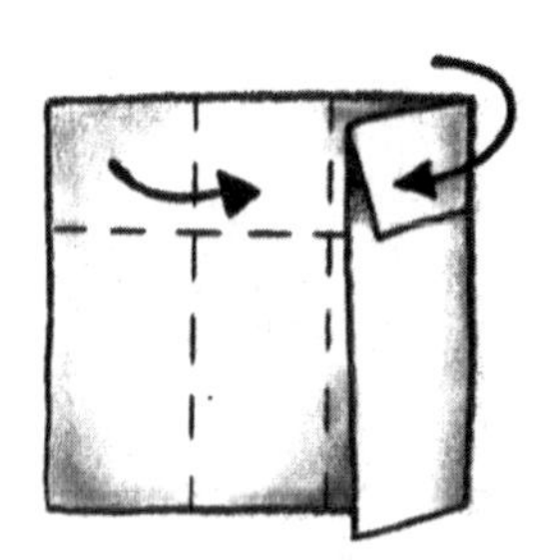

3 Fold each short side of the paper to the middle.

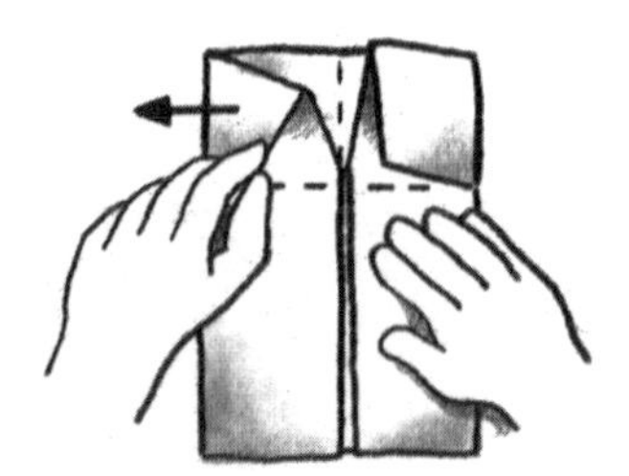

4 Grab the bottom right corner of the square at the top of the left side of the paper. Begin pulling the corner to the left, past the edge of the paper to make a triangle.

5 Press the triangle flat. Repeat on the other side: Grab the bottom left corner of the square at the top of the right side of the paper and pull to the right.

6 Turn the paper over. Glue buttons to the roof of the house. Glue the paper doily to the front of the house. Decorate with House Trims, if you like (see page 32). Glue a photograph on top of the paper doily.

Cinnamon Popcorn

Share a bowl of this snack with your best buddy.

What you'll need...

- 2 tablespoons margarine, melted
- ¼ teaspoon ground cinnamon
- 4 cups popped popcorn
- 1 cup bite-size graham crackers with cinnamon-sugar topping
- ½ cup candy-coated peanut-butter-flavored pieces

1 In a small bowl use a spoon to stir together the melted margarine and cinnamon. Put the popcorn in a large bowl. Pour the margarine with cinnamon over the popcorn (see photo). Stir the popcorn to mix it with the margarine and cinnamon.

2 Stir the graham crackers and candy into the popcorn mixture (see photo). Store in a covered container. Makes about 5 cups.

Friendship Chain

Trade links with your friends so each of you can make a chain.

What you'll need...

- Scissors
- Construction paper
- Chain Decorations (see page 32)
- Tape or white crafts glue

1 For the links of the chain, cut strips of construction paper about 12 inches long and 2 to 3 inches wide (see photo).

2 Decorate each paper strip with Chain Decorations (see photo and page 32).

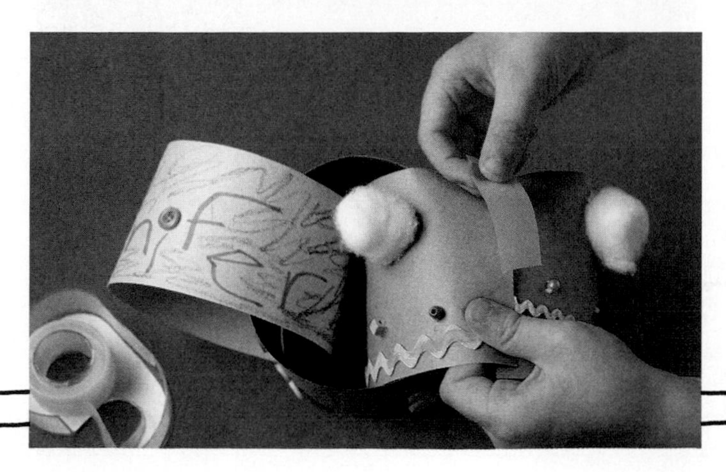

3 To make the chain, tape the ends of 1 paper strip together to make a circle. Then, take a second paper strip and put it through the circle. Tape the ends together to make another circle (see photo). Repeat until all of the paper strips have been used.

MORE FROM Max

Picture Frame House

You can use your house as a picture frame or just as a house. Either way, try some of these decorating ideas.

House Trims: Color the house with crayons or markers. Add a door and windows, if you like. Then glue on beads, lace, rick-rack, pipe cleaners, or yarn.

You can add a bow or a candy-cane decoration to the frame. Use a paper punch to punch two holes near the top of the house. Then thread yarn or ribbon through the holes. Or, push a small candy cane through the holes.

Cinnamon Popcorn

People have been eating popcorn for a very long time. It's a good treat to share with friends. Make the sharing more fun by serving the popcorn in a special basket (see photo, page 28).

Line a plastic berry basket with a brightly colored napkin. Attach a pipe cleaner to the basket for a handle. Weave ribbons through the holes in the sides of the basket, if you like. Then fill the basket with Cinnamon Popcorn (page 29) or Dive-In Caramel Corn.

Dive-In Caramel Corn

- 3 tablespoons margarine or butter
- ¼ cup corn syrup
- 1 tablespoon molasses
- 6 cups popped popcorn
- 1 cup dry-roasted peanuts, cashews, or sunflower nuts

- With adult help, melt the margarine or butter in a small saucepan. Remove the pan from heat. Stir in corn syrup and molasses.
- Put the popcorn in a 13x9x2-inch baking pan. Drizzle the molasses-syrup mixture over the popcorn, stirring to cover the popcorn with the mixture.
- Bake in a 325° oven about 15 minutes, stirring twice. With adult help, transfer hot mixture to a bowl. Stir in peanuts. Store in a tightly covered container at room temperature. Makes 4 cups.

Friendship Chain

Here's how a paper chain becomes a Friendship Chain. Ask your friends to decorate some paper strips. Then have each person trade a paper strip for someone else's paper strip. When everyone is done trading, they each make a Friendship Chain. Each chain should have one paper strip, or link, from each person.

Chain Decorations: You can use any of these ideas to decorate your paper strips. (Or, make up your own.)

Start with paint, crayons, or markers. Then glue on cotton balls, buttons, dried beans or peas, uncooked macaroni, fabric, or lace.

BETTER HOMES AND GARDENS® BOOKS
Editor: Gerald M. Knox Art Director: Ernest Shelton Managing Editor: David A. Kirchner
Department Head, Family Life: Sharyl Heiken
A TREE FULL OF FRIENDS
Editors: Jennifer Darling and Sandra Granseth Graphic Designers: Brenda Lesch and Linda Vermie
Editorial Project Manager: Angela K. Renkoski
Contributing Writer: Jane Stanley Contributing Illustrator: Buck Jones
Contributing Color Artist: Sue Fitzpatrick Cornelison Contributing Photographer: Scott Little